Malice in Manila

THE JEALOUSY OF A SISTER RAN SO DEEP
THAT SHE BECAME AN ACTIVE PARTICIPANT
IN HER BROTHER-IN-LAW'S MURDER PLOT.

HANIF MIKE KARIM

authorHOUSE®

AuthorHouse™
1663 Liberty Drive
Bloomington, IN 47403
www.authorhouse.com
Phone: 833-262-8899

Published by AuthorHouse 12/16/2020

ISBN: 978-1-6655-0423-2 (sc)
ISBN: 978-1-6655-0424-9 (hc)
ISBN: 978-1-6655-0425-6 (e)

Library of Congress Control Number: 2020920171

This book is dedicated to my mother, Halima Bai, with deep gratitude for raising me single-handedly after the passing of my dad when I was four years old. Also to my beautiful wife, Nuzhat, who has always believed in me throughout all my endeavors.

Contents

Chapter 1

Sohail and Rebecca had been high school sweethearts. He had not forgotten even after almost forty years how Rebecca had helped him, when he was first admitted to their high school. He was not just new to the school but also new to the country. His skin color, his name, and the language barrier had been enough for the class bullies to embarrass and make fun of him. He used to think of Rebecca as his angel and could not get her out of his mind day and night.

That was back then. How times had changed.

There were times lately when they could not stand each other. Other times, they barely tolerated each other. Their marriage had not been on a strong footing for quite some time.

Sohail Kolsy had recently retired from an executive position at a large bank and was fully enjoying alarm-clock-free retired life, but Rebecca was still working as a manager at a women's clothing design company. It was a stressful job that required a lot of traveling and long hours, but she still enjoyed its challenges and the company's success. Unlike Sohail, she would not even think about retiring.

Sohail and Rebecca had a son and a daughter—Salim, thirty-seven, and Sameera, thirty-five. They also had four grandkids, who were a tremendous joy for them and a big reason for their still being together, after all the tumultuous years of bitterness and fights. Salim and Sameera were aware of their parents' frictions over the years, but they tried not to interfere.

They had very few friends, but they had been good friends with one couple, Josh and Katie, for many years. They enjoyed one another's company and often got together. It also helped that they didn't live far from one another. Josh owned an established real estate company with about half a dozen employees, and Katie was a happy housewife. They didn't have any kids.

One evening, when the two couples were together at Josh and Katie's house, things turned unusually ugly. Rebecca seemed a little more stressed out than usual. She told the group that she had to get up early the next morning and catch an early flight to New Orleans to attend a seminar. Since Josh had arranged this get-together while coordinating with Sohail, he looked at Sohail with a surprised look as if to ask, *Why didn't you say anything?*

"*Don't look at me, I didn't know anything about it myself,*" Sohail told Josh.

"*I didn't say anything to him because he doesn't care anyway,*" Rebecca remarked snidely.

"*Excuse me. That wasn't a very nice thing to say in front of the company,*" Sohail said.

"*Sohail, stop pretending. They're our close friends. It's not as if they don't know.*"

"*I agree that they're our close friends, but you don't have to be such a loudmouth in front of them.*"

"*Now you're calling me a loudmouth? Is that a nice thing, Mr. Nice Guy?*"

"*Who started it?*"

Josh tried to intervene, but Rebecca was not having it.

"*He always wants to pretend like he was an angel, but he's not. I know the reality. Only I know how difficult it is to live with him and his hypocrisy.*"

"*Look, I just told Josh I didn't know you had travel plans, and if that bent you out of shape, it's not my fault. You were probably hiding it from me because your friend Shelton*" *was going to be there again."* This time it was Sohail's turn to throw a jab.

"I don't need to hide anything from you. Yes, he is going to be there. Do what you want, think what you want—I don't give a shit!" Rebecca got angrier.

"Hey, go ahead, do whatever you want. It's your life." Sohail gave up.

Josh and Katie were sitting there looking at each other, not daring to interrupt. It wasn't the first time they had seen this kind of a spat between the two.

It got a little quieter after that commotion. The evening was pretty much over.

After Sohail and Rebecca left, Katie and Josh discussed what they had just witnessed; they had their own opinions about the fight. Katie thought that Sohail should be more sensitive to Rebecca's needs, but Josh thought Rebecca was too aggressive and didn't respect Sohail at all. They agreed to disagree and left it at that.

When Rebecca and Sohail got home, it was not over.

"Why do you have to be so nasty in front of other people?" Sohail asked.

"I told you, I don't consider them as other people. They already know everything. I don't like to pretend like you do. You were brought up like that—I wasn't."

"There you go again. All my life, you've taunted me about how I was brought up. You don't ever give up, do you?"

"Look, Sohail, I have to get up early. I don't have the time, the energy, or the desire to continue this stupid discussion. Nothing is going to change anyway. I have to go to sleep," Rebecca said as she walked to another room.

"Go to hell. See if I care," Sohail said; he had had enough.

Rebecca heard that. *"That's my point. You don't care."*

A few months after that incident, Rebecca filed for divorce.

Josh and Katie were not surprised. Salim and Sameera had known about the problems and the possibility of divorce, but it was still not easy to see it finally happening.

Josh was closer to Sohail than Katie was to Rebecca. The two men often talked. They discussed all matters big or small going on in their lives and depended on each other for sincere advice.

"It was something that was bound to happen, and it finally did. What can I say?" Sohail was withdrawn.

Josh tried to cheer him up. *"Look at it this way, Sohail. You knew it was going to happen sooner or later, and now you don't have to wait. You still have your grandkids to enjoy. Just chill and let things calm down. How are Salim and Sameera taking it?"*

"They're telling me the same thing, that it was bound to happen. My suspicions about Shelton were correct. She moved in with him right away."

"Oh wow. That was fast. That makes you wonder if she already had plans in place." Even Josh was surprised.

"Of course she had everything planned. She's no dummy. She doesn't believe in wasting any time. I didn't like the guy the first time I saw him."

"Amazing. You'd think that people would slow down a little after a certain age. But no, some people don't even know what slowing down means." Josh tried to console Sohail.

"Oh well. It is what it is. Some things you can't control."

"All right, Sohail, take care. Call me if you need anything."

"Yeah, talk to you later."

Chapter 2

After the breakup of his marriage, Sohail lost interest in everything he used to enjoy. He stopped going to the gym. He used to go for a round of golf every once in a while, but he stopped that too. His outlook on life in general had also changed noticeably. His confidence became shaky as far as socializing was concerned.

Josh turned out to be the only friend who kept in touch with him. Sohail noticed that not only had his acquaintances stopped contacting him, but also even those he had considered friends were not too anxious to console him.

Even his son and daughter talked to him only when he took the initiative to call them. He was terribly hurt that they had seemed to have taken their mother's side in spite of the fact that she was the one who had been having an affair. He had expected more from Salim and Sameera. He had expected that they would bring the grandkids to him more often, knowing that he was alone and lonely, but that hadn't happened.

Only Josh knew how depressed and hurt he was with his son's and daughter's attitude toward him.

"Don't worry, Sohail. Things will turn around," Josh would encourage him. *"Statistics show that the kids always gravitate toward the mother after the parents' divorce."*

"Fuck the statistics. They aren't kids. They're grown-ups. They should know better about what happened. I can't believe it. My faith in them is evaporating by the minute. I thought I had raised them better than that. I'd always emphasized fairness and thoughtfulness. This is a lesson I'll never forget. Who knew? The least they could had done was to treat both parents equally." Sohail would

vent, and Josh, a loyal friend, would show his understanding and make him believe that he knew how frustrated he was.

ONE YEAR LATER.

Things were starting to change somewhat. Sohail was beginning to come out of his shell. His relationship with Salim and Sameera was beginning to improve a bit, and Josh remained a steady, loyal friend. He would visit Sohail often to keep him company. They genuinely enjoyed spending time together, picking each other's brains, and talking about everything, including politics, religion, women, and kids.

They had different political affiliations, but they always respected each other's opinions. Sohail, an immigrant, had more sympathy for people in need. He felt that it was the government's job to use tax dollars wisely. Good government meant to him spending money not only appropriately but also with compassion.

Josh on the other hand strongly believed that all able-bodied people needed to be self-reliant and not look for government handouts. He believed that people became complacent and dependent too easily. In his opinion, government help that came too quickly took away the incentive to look harder. He thought government should step in only after all the available resources had been used up. If that was not done, he believed, people would become trapped in a cycle that was hard to get out of. He also believed that too many people were milking the system.

One time, Sohail asked Josh, *"Come on, man—how many people do you know personally who are milking the system?"*

"I don't know any. I don't hang around with that crowd, but that's not the point. I read the paper, read the statistics, and listen to the news," Josh replied.

"I believe with all my heart that human beings are

basically decent. Unless they don't have a choice, they don't want handouts. However, they do need to feed their families." That would always be Sohail's default position.

"Sohail, I've never been against helping people who deserve help, such as the elderly or people with special needs, but I can't see my tax dollars going to people who don't want to make an effort to help themselves. That's charity. I should be able to decide for myself whom I want to give charity to. I don't want the government to decide on my behalf."

"That's where we disagree. How is it even possible for the government to go around asking people what charities they want to contribute to? Come on, man, be reasonable." Sometimes Sohail would show frustration.

"Look, you and I disagree fundamentally on a few things, and we always will. Some people are born that way, congenitally deceiving people, and they can't stop even if they wanted to." Josh was adamant.

"I don't agree with you. God's fair."

"I beg your pardon. Think again. Do you really think life is fair? I can give you thousands of examples to prove that it isn't."

That statement would always make Sohail scratch his head. He knew Josh was right about that. In their discussions about life not being fair, Josh had always won that argument.

When Josh saw Sohail being so quiet, he started babbling. *"If God is always present everywhere and he's fair, why is there so much inequality in the world? Some people are billionaires while others don't have enough to eat. Why are there so many natural disasters and mostly in poor countries? So many innocent children are killed in those disasters. What is their fault? So many people are born with disabilities, some are born blind, and others have never walked. What's their fault?"* Josh was going on and on until Sohail tried to stop him.

"Okay, okay, I get your point."

Josh continued, *"Now let me guess what you're going to say, Sohail. Every time this topic is raised, you and others like you always say one of two things. One, that God works in mysterious ways. We don't know his reasons, and we shouldn't question his judgments. He is almighty and leave it that. Just have faith in his judgments. Two, that he's testing us. People who suffer in this world will be rewarded in the next world. Am I right?"*

Sohail shook his head. He saw no point in going on further. He did however say under his breath, *"Can't argue with somebody who has lost his faith in God."*

"I heard that, Sohail."

"I probably never told you this before, but there was a time when I was very religious. I didn't lose my faith suddenly. It was gradual." Josh became very emotional; his eyes were almost moist.

Sohail had not seen that side of Josh. *"What? What happened?"* Looking straight into his eyes.

"You know Sohail, you're lucky to have two kids. Katie and I have always missed knowing what it was like to be parents. So many times, we have felt the emptiness in our lives as if they weren't complete. We just don't know how it feels to be a parent."

"Katie and I tried everything. We went to half a dozen doctors and even to a fertility masseuse. We researched our church's stance on in-vitro fertilization. The Catholic Church considers artificial insemination morally unacceptable, but the chaplain assured us that we were doing God's will by building a family.

"Katie endured a physically taxing, emotionally draining

gauntlet of needles and doctors' visits. One doctor even retrieved her eggs, fertilized, and implanted them. She got pictures of the growing embryo. Yet the pregnancy failed. Nothing worked. It was hard to figure out God's plan for us. That's when we raged at God and our faith became very shaky."

Sohail had never seen this side of Josh before. He wanted to help his friend, but there was absolutely nothing he could do.

Josh went on. *"You know my parents had eight kids, and Katie has seven siblings. When we were younger, it was hard for us to be around friends and families with kids."*

"Look, Josh my friend, having children is not all that rosy. Sure, you enjoy them when they're young, but man, the sleepless nights, raising them when they're going to school. You name it. The doctors, the dentists—It's not that easy. Look at my own situation. Where are they when I need them? Nowhere to be found. Many times, you feel you're better off without them. Believe me, I think most parents feel that way."

It was getting late. Josh wanted to leave. *"Sure, it's not easy, but at least you experienced it. We didn't. We thought about adopting, but that never materialized. Oh well. It wasn't meant to be."*

Chapter 3

Sohail was slowly coming around and opening up to the idea of socializing and even dating again. Josh, sensing that change in Sohail's attitude, fixed him up with a couple of dates, but those efforts didn't go very far; Sohail was too rigid in his ways.

Sohail had started developing certain strong opinions about American women. He thought they were generally more aggressive than his comfort zone would allow for. He also started forming new opinions about women in general and particularly women who were too independent. He started wondering why so many women were dissatisfied with their marriages. He thought that too often these women were second-guessing themselves even after they got married. They were not sure if they had made the right choice or thought they could had done better.

He was tilting more and more towards getting involved with only non-American women. He was convinced that he should get involved only with somebody who was not too independent minded. He liked the concept of the couple depending on each other. As time passed, this conviction got stronger. He had a lasting bitter taste of what had happened in his marriage. It had made him totally insecure.

He spent hours researching successful and unsuccessful relationship models and why so many marriages failed, particularly in Western societies. The more he studied this subject, the more he came to realize that in the West, couples did not rely much on each other. Material things were easily disposable, and human relationships were easily replaceable. Husbands and wives had their egos to deal with, and they wanted to get the upper hand, be the bosses in their relationships in subtle ways without saying so.

Sohail had worked in the corporate world for many years. He knew that in any structure, there had to be only one person at the top who made the big decisions. If there were more than one person making the big decisions, there was always conflict. He was surprised as well as upset at himself that it had taken him so long to understand such a simple phenomenon. He also understood that in some societies, women were suppressed and made no decisions. He was not interested in looking at those models. He did not believe in those crazy philosophies.

Sohail had heard of pen pals for many years but had never tried it. He decided to experiment with that concept. He got in touch with some interesting women from other countries but had no luck in finding anyone special.

Then he looked into the mail-order bride business; this was a totally new phenomenon for him which he had heard of only recently. He was trying everything, so he decided to give that a shot as well. He wanted to approach it carefully and methodically.

Again, he contacted women from different countries including Japan, Russia, India, Thailand, and the Philippines. In his research, he had found that those countries were most frequently mentioned in that business.

His research showed him that there were many reasons why a woman from the Philippines would be best suited for his temperament and personality.

He found out that women from the Philippines could be contacted via Skype and FaceTime. Talking face to face would make it easier for both parties to determine their compatibility. Filipino women were not high maintenance as were women from other countries, and there was no language barrier because English was the spoken language in the Philippines. They preferred older men to younger men because they were more concerned with financial security than with looks. They felt that older men were more dependable and therefore offered less of a chance that they would cheat on them. There were other good reasons.

From that point on, Sohail focused on meeting only somebody from Philippines.

After an extensive search, he found what he thought was a perfect match for him —Catalina. She was thirty-seven and had an eight-year-old daughter, Karina.

"What is a nice girl like you doing on the mail-order bride site?" Sohail asked when they first spoke.

"It wasn't my choice. It's what my parents wanted. They are poor, I have a daughter, and we live with them. They are supporting us, so I abide by their rules."

Sohail appreciated her frank answer.

"But don't you tell your parents that you feel embarrassed by that label of mail-order bride?"

"I used to be, but not anymore. You don't understand— there are more important things in my life that I have to worry about, than this label. It's more important that my daughter and I have a roof over our heads, and my parents are providing us that roof right now. We're grateful for that. You see, beggars can't be choosers."

Sohail liked Catalina's simple and honest approach to life; he thought it was refreshing. They spoke with each other regularly for several months.

When Sohail told Josh about it, he laughed at the mere mention of the words *mail-order bride*. When he stopped laughing and realized Sohail was serious, he thought he had gone nuts.

"Man, there are so many women out there who want a family and would love to get hooked up with a stable guy.

Why do you have to go to the other side of the world? And then a mail-order bride?" Josh ridiculed him.

"Look, Josh. I've spent a lot of time looking into this. What motivates men and women is totally different. You and I have had this discussion many times. I don't think there's any other way for me."

Sohail kept going, *"Catalina is perfect for me. I don't think I'll find a more suitable person than her. She seems kind, caring, and genuine. She has assured me over and over that our age difference will never be a factor. I just want to believe her. My gut tells me she's telling the truth."* Sohail sounded so sure about it.

"How can you be so sure? You've never even met the woman. What if she was just saying those things to win you over and will become a monster once you're hooked?"

"Obviously I cannot be a hundred percent sure, but that's the chance I'm willing to take."

Josh tried his best to talk him out of it; he thought it was ridiculous way of thinking, but Sohail had made up his mind.

Sohail then told his son and daughter about his plans, and their reaction was even worse than Josh's; they thought the old man had lost his marbles. They were worried about what people would think if they found out that their dad had married a mail-order bride half his age.

Chapter 4

Sohail and Catalina kept in touch on Skype and FaceTime. It got to the point that they were talking to each other every day. Karina was also getting attached to Sohail; she would call him Nanapapa, and he loved that.

"When are you coming here to live with us, Nanapapa?" Karina asked him all the time.

"Soon, very soon," Sohail would say.

Catalina had warned Sohail that her parents had gotten the whiff that something serious was going on between them and that they wanted to know about it.

"What should I tell them, Sohail? I hope you're as serious about this whole thing as we are."

"Just tell them we're very serious."

"Are you okay with coming to the Philippines and giving them some money? They will expect that."

"How much money are we talking about?"

"At least six or seven thousand dollars."

"I'll bring that amount with me."

Sohail was hoping he could get Josh to go with him; he thought it would be too awkward going alone. Josh was not only reluctant; he also thought it was foolish. Sohail tried everything he could to get Josh to change his mind, including offering to pay his expenses for the trip.

"What have you got to lose, man? You aren't the one getting married. I am. I'm taking the chance, not you. You can't take a few days off for me? What kind of a friend are you?" Sohail would tease Josh.

"Look, Sohail, I'm capable of doing a lot more than that for a friend, but this just doesn't jibe with me. I can't see a friend deliberately going into a ditch and be a bystander."

15

"Josh, why don't you understand that human beings are basically nice? I intend to give her and Karina so much love and care that she wouldn't even think about leaving or deceiving me. Why can't you understand that? Why would she bite the hand that fed her?"

"She will be coming to a new country, a country that everybody loves to come to. My research shows that Filipinos love to come to United States more so than any other country. It is supposed to be very prestigious for them. Catalina and her daughter will be totally dependent on me for everything. I just don't know how to make you understand."

"Look, Sohail, those are all logical reasons, but some people are beyond understanding logic, and I think that you cannot expect a mail-order bride to understand logic," Josh would argue.

"Josh, I'm telling you she's not like that. She's an educated woman. It's just that she's going through some unfortunate circumstances."

"Of course I don't know her, but I know that some people are born evil. They don't know the difference between good and bad and are ready to do whatever is necessary to harm you and take advantage of you. They have no conscience or sense of appreciation. They get some kind of sick pleasure out of harming and hurting people. I'm not saying your woman is like that, but are you willing to take the chance of finding out she is after you're tied up with her?"

"Yes! That's what I've been trying to tell you all along. I've made that decision. I'm willing to take that chance." Sohail was determined.

After having tried his best and Sohail not relenting, Josh gave up.

"I tell you what. I'm willing to bet that if you marry her, it won't last longer than seven years at the most, and I think it could be even shorter than that. If you last that long, I'll give you ten thousand dollars. If you lose, you pay me that amount." Josh was confident he will win.

"I agree, Josh, on two conditions. You go with me to the Philippines, and nobody knows about our bet, including our wives."

"You're on, Sohail!" Josh agreed.

THE BET WAS ON.

Chapter 5

Catalina, Karina, and her mother and father greeted Sohail and Josh at the airport.

The two were pleasantly surprised. Everyone was so nice, polite, and hospitable. They made Sohail and Josh comfortable as if they were long-lost friends. Karina kept hugging Sohail as if she had known him forever thanks to Skype and FaceTime.

Catalina had prepared Sohail's favorite dishes; after having talked to Sohail for months, she knew what he liked. They had discussed every other subject in the world as well as food.

After the meal, they had dessert and a few drinks. Even Josh, who had been skeptical, was impressed by their hospitality and the absence of any awkward feeling. Yet Josh couldn't shake the thought that they were having dinner at a mail-order bride's home.

Whenever Sohail and Catalina got a chance, they stole glances at each other. Whenever Sohail got a chance, he would squeeze her hand. They felt like teenagers. That didn't go unnoticed by Catalina's parents and Josh. Catalina's parents motioned Catalina to take Sohail into the other room for some privacy. Catalina got the hint and did just that.

"So how do you feel, Mr. Sohail Kolsy?" Catalina joked when they got some privacy.

"Oh so now I'm Mr. Sohail Kolsy, huh? Since when have you started calling me that, Miss Catalina?"

They laughed and hugged.

"I am so happy, Catalina. You are more beautiful in person than in video images and the photographs."

Catalina became bashful and embarrassed by his open, generous, and genuine compliments. *"You are so nice. What do you think of Karina? You know she's the most important person in my life."*

"I adore her. She's such a delight and so sweet. She already seems to have bonded with me. I can't believe it. I definitely underestimated the power of Skype and FaceTime."

"Sohail, I can't tell you how happy I am to hear that from you. I hope you really mean it."

"Of course I mean it. You'll find out sooner than later that I don't say things I don't mean."

"One more thing, Sohail. I've told you this before, but I want to tell you again. My father has asked both of my sisters and their husbands to come over and meet you tomorrow. Please don't mind my younger sister's attitude. She's very unpredictable and handful, I just want to warn you."

"Don't you worry. I'll handle her. Thanks for reminding me. I'd forgotten about her."

Then they went back and joined the others.

Sohail and Josh stayed as long as they could before heading to their hotel. They were tired after the long flight. They promised to come back the next day.

Chapter 6

When Sohail and Josh went back to Catalina's place the next day, the house seemed full of people. Catalina's sisters, Leona and Yvonne, were there with their husbands, Carlos and Miguel, and their kids. Everybody was introduced to Sohail and Josh.

Catalina was worried about Leona's uppity attitude and particularly about her tendency to get jealous and boss everyone around. Sohail noticed that she keenly checked him out when they were introduced and was not as friendly as the others were. She even asked some rude questions.

"So Sohail, Catalina told us that you have two children."

"Yes I do."

"That's nice. How old are they?"

Sohail wasn't expecting that question; he glanced at Catalina. But after having been warned about Leona's nature, he said, *"Thirty-seven and thirty-five."*

"Oh, that's about the same age as Catalina."

"That's right, but Catalina knows all about that. You don't have to worry about it." Sohail was getting a bit ticked.

"Do they have kids?" Leona continued to have fun at his expense.

"Yeah, they both have two kids."

"So you're the grandpa of four kids already, Wow. How nice!"

Leona soon realized that she was getting out of line. Her father also gave her a stern look. Joseph, Catalina's father, wanted to get Sohail away from Leona. He asked Sohail and Josh to come with him to another room so they could talk privately. Sohail was relieved to get away from Leona.

When they went into another room, Joseph got right to the point.

"Well, Sohail, now that you've met Catalina and Karina in person, what are your thoughts? Do you want some more time to think about it, or you want to proceed with the next step? As her father, I want to make sure she and her daughter are happy wherever they go."

"I can tell you without hesitation, Joseph, that I have fallen in love with your daughter. You can rest assured. I have come here so that we could meet each other in person, and I can show you my seriousness and sincerity."

"I hope Catalina has conveyed my message to you that I am in a financial bind and would need some monetary help," Joseph nervously stated.

"Yes, don't worry. Catalina had told me that, and I have brought the money with me."

The old man was so overwhelmed that he immediately hugged Sohail and with tearful eyes said, *"Welcome to my family."*

He then unabashedly took Sohail's hand and dragged him to the room where the rest of the family was. His cheerful entrance told the others everything; they had been anticipating this outcome. They were all smiles, and the congratulated Catalina and Sohail. Even Leona managed to smile a little. Joseph then proceeded to instruct Catalina, Sohail, and Josh to get ready to go to the courthouse for the marriage license and certificate.

The justice of the peace at the court house performed his duty and declared Sohail and Catalina husband and wife. The whole process went smoothly, and Sohail and Catalina kissed for the first time. The court issued them a marriage certificate. Sohail knew that it was the most important piece of paper that he would need to file for Catalina's and Karina's visas.

They went home, and everyone was in a celebratory mood—Music was blasting, the smells of delicious food were prevalent, and the adults were drinking. The kids were running around; they didn't know much about what was going on, but they knew something good was happening since all the adults were happy and drinking.

Karina was the cheerleader among the kids.

Everyone respected the fact that this was a particularly special occasion for Catalina and Sohail, and they knew Sohail was leaving the next day, so they gave them the maximum privacy.

Catalina and Sohail ended up in the same room where they had been the day before.

"I'm so happy, Sohail. I hope I can make you happy and come up to your expectations as a wife." Catalina was beaming with joy.

"Sweetheart, I don't have big expectations. I'm an average man. I just want us to have a nice and peaceful life together with our child. I am aware we both had some rough times in the past and will have to go through some challenges. I'm taking the responsibility of bringing you and Karina to a new country and starting a new life. You will have the challenge of assimilating into a new culture and learn a lot of new things. Karina will have a new school and new friends to deal with. But we'll all prevail if we love each other and take care of each other."

Catalina was so overwhelmed with what Sohail had said that she just hugged him tightly without saying anything. With that, they went back and joined the others.

At the airport before departure, Sohail assured Catalina and Joseph that he would immediately start the paperwork process for Catalina's and Karina's visas. Catalina's eyes were welling up with tears. Joseph pressed Sohail's hand with his eyes telling him not to forget his promise.

During the flight home, Sohail tried to get Josh's impression of the whole thing,

"Josh, so now you agree that I made the right decision. You met everybody. Weren't they nice? Come on, admit it."

"Yes, they were all nice, but there's a huge difference between being nice and having a good marriage. You're not marrying the family, you are marrying just one person."

"I agree, but you also met Catalina. Don't you think she's nice?"

"She seems very nice, but Sohail, your and my ways of making decisions are much different. I wouldn't have made such an important decision based on some Skype meetings. In my mind, there's too much at stake. I sincerely hope that you've made the right decision and that you don't regret it. We are all different and we have our own way of handling things."

Josh had softened his stance on the whole bizarre decision Sohail had made, but he was still very skeptical and thought his bet was safe.

Sohail had promised Catalina that he would call her as soon as he got home, and he could hardly wait to do that.

"Hi, sweetie. I'm home."

"How was the flight?" Catalina was thrilled to hear from him.

"Long. I miss you already."

"Oh Sohail, really? All you have to do is Skype me if you want to see me."

"No, it's not the same now that I've seen you in person. It won't satisfy my thirst. You look so much better in person, and I won't be able to hug you," Sohail teased her.

"So how does it feel being a married man again and having a child?"

"It feels great. I can hardly wait until you two are here."

"Me too, Sohail. You better go and rest. You must be tired after the long flight."

"You're right. I am a little tired. I'll talk to you soon. Love you."

Within a few days, Sohail started the paperwork he needed to bring his new family to the States. He even hired a lawyer to expedite things and make sure nothing fell through the cracks. He kept in touch with Catalina and updated her on her immigration status.

Chapter 7

With Sohail's diligence and with the lawyer's help, the immigration process went smoothly; Catalina's and Karina's visas came through within nine months, quicker than Sohail had expected. His decision to hire a lawyer had paid off.

On the day of their departure from the Philippines, Catalina was extremely anxious and nervous. The only thing Karina knew was that she was going to fly in a plane. Catalina's parents had mixed emotions about their daughter and granddaughter leaving; they were worried but hopeful that they would start a new and a better life. They gave them their blessings and hoped for the best.

Sohail brought Josh and Katie to the airport to welcome Catalina and Karina. Catalina was hoping that Sohail's son and daughter would also come to greet them, but they weren't there.

Sohail introduced Catalina to Katie. She already knew Josh.

"How was the flight?" Katie asked.

"Long and a bit tiring, but otherwise, everything went well. Karina slept most of the way."

Sohail was hugging and kissing Karina, who was by then wide awake and was trying to figure out where she was and who this lady in the car with Mama and Nanapapa and Josh was.

After Sohail dropped off Josh and Katie, he drove home. Catalina was super pleased to see how nice and big the house was.

"Welcome home!" Sohail hugged and kissed Catalina. *"How do you like it?"*

Catalina responded by giving him a kiss in return. *"Does that answer your question?"*

Sohail nodded. He then gave them the grand tour of his two-story, five-bedroom house. Catalina wanted to see every nook and cranny and loved every bit of it. Sohail had picked a room for Karina, who was equally wide eyed and thrilled; she had never had a room of her own before. Sohail saw that the girl was trying to understand that concept. *A whole room belonging to just her alone? Of course she loves it*, he thought.

"*How did you manage such a big house all by yourself, Sohail?*"

"*I had help, but now I have you.*"

That brought a smile to Catalina's face.

"*This is where all three of us are going to start our new life, dear.*" Sohail said.

Catalina nodded; she couldn't hide her happiness.

A month later, Sohail arranged a small get-together at the house to introduce his new family. He invited a few close friends and the loved ones, including Josh and Katie, Salim, Sameera and their families. Catalina was particularly nervous about meeting with Sohail's kids for the first time and was hoping to make a good impression on them. The food was catered.

While most of the guests welcomed the newcomers, Sohail's son and daughter were surprisingly not so friendly. They were acting strangely and were downright rude. Their rudeness and disrespect got to the point where she couldn't take it anymore. She went to her bedroom and started crying. Sohail had been watching the interaction between Salim and Sameera and Catalina; he very much wanted the three to at least get along and *hopefully like each other*, but that was apparently not in the cards. When he saw Catalina leave for the bedroom, he told Salim and Sameera that he wanted to talk to them privately.

He led them to the bedroom where Catalina was, closed the door, and screamed, "*What the hell do you think you two are doing?*" He glared at them. "*If you think I'm going to accept this behavior toward my wife, you're sadly mistaken. Let me make it as clear as I can—Catalina is here to stay. She is not only my wife. She's also the queen of this house."*

His son and daughter had not been expecting such an outburst from their father. They knew he was still angry about his divorce and unhappy with the way their mother had handled the situation, but they hadn't known he was *that* angry. They had no clue that their father had expected more support from them after the divorce.

Sohail commanded, *"I want both of you apologize to Catalina right now or get out of our house."*

That was another shock. Sameera stormed out of the room slamming the door and mumbling that she would never come back. She immediately left the party with her family. Salim also left quietly but without saying anything.

Sohail hugged Catalina and apologized for his son's and daughter's behavior. *"I didn't raise them to act like that."*

Catalina was so impressed and overwhelmed with the way he had handled the situation that she gave him a big hug. *"Sohail, I can't believe you've been so nice to me."*

"What do mean nice to you? You better get used to it. You're my wife, and everyone has to treat you with respect—I don't care who it is."

"But I don't want to come in between you and your family."

"Catalina, don't forget this—you and Karina are my primary family now. Sameera and Salim are grown-ups with their own families. They must learn to respect you or they won't be welcome here."

"They already didn't like me. Now they'll probably hate me even more."

"Catalina, don't worry about it. They'll come around. They need to know that they can't disrespect you. If I hadn't let them know that now, they'd do it again. I know how to handle them. I raised them. They're my kids."

She thanked him profusely for the way he was taking care of her.

They returned to their guests. Everybody was having fun specially Karina and the other kids. Catalina mingled with everyone; and with her easygoing nature, it wasn't hard for her to make new friends. Everybody had a good time and enjoyed themselves.

Sohail and Catalina made sure Karina quickly settled into her new school. They knew she was a bright kid and would have no problem resuming where she had left off in Manila. She already had the language skills. Karina was happy and was making friends all the time, and they were inviting her for sleepovers, pajama parties, birthdays, and whatnot. She was having a ball, and in no time, she forgot all about Manila.

Sohail was as enthusiastic about starting a new family as Catalina was. He treated Karina like a little princess; he met all her needs and loved doing that. Karina was still calling him Nanapapa, which he totally adored.

Although Sohail missed seeing his own grandchildren, Karina had more or less filled that vacuum. Sameera had broken off all contact with Sohail; Salim was still in touch but to a much lesser degree than when Sohail had been married to his mother. Catalina realized that, but there wasn't much she could do. She felt bad that because of her, Sohail had been alienated by his own family, but whenever she tried to talk to Sohail about that, he stopped her.

Sohail knew that his kids will never understand what it was like to have been cheated on by their mother at his age. He was also convinced that his kids were selfish. *They just think about themselves and never really try to figure out what their father went through*, he thought. Sohail was also the type who didn't feel comfortable bad-mouthing their mother behind her back; he knew that would backfire and make the situation worse.

A year later, Catalina had passed the written driving test and was taking driving lessons from a professional instructor. She was so happy and often thought about how her life had changed for the better. Whenever she talked to or Skyped with her parents, she thanked them for hooking her up with a good man like Sohail. Although Sohail and Catalina had found each other; the parents had had nothing to do with that, but she still gave them the credit to make them feel good. After all, her parents had given her their blessings.

She often mentioned to them about how everybody had thought she had been the unluckiest among the sisters, but that hadn't turned out to be the case. She had become the lucky one. She was in a mansion in the United States living like a queen with such a doting husband, nice cars, and a nice neighborhood. Her daughter was so happy going to a great school; she had her own room and was being driven everywhere by her devoted stepfather. *What else could a woman ask for?* she wondered.

"We are all so happy for you. Just take care of yourself and Karina. Don't worry about us," her mom and dad would say whenever she expressed her guilt about her luxurious life while they were struggling.

Everybody in Manila was happy to hear that Catalina was living a good life in the United States except one person—her younger sister, Leona. Outwardly, she would go along with everyone and express her happiness for her sister, but she was still jealous. She hadn't liked Sohail from the get-go, and she had been jealous of her sister all her life.

The two-couple get-togethers Sohail and his ex used to have with Josh and Katie started again with Catalina replacing Rebecca, but they met only at Sohail and Catalina's house rather than restaurants; Sohail and Catalina didn't like leaving Karina with a babysitter. An advantage to this new arrangement was that they got to try exotic Filipino dishes Catalina prepared, and everyone loved Catalina's cooking.

Katie told Josh, *"I can't believe this man has changed so much. Look at how nice he is now compared to when he was married to Rebecca. He was always so cutting, narcissistic, and sarcastic. I didn't think he was even capable of changing."*

Josh of course didn't agree with Katie about Sohail being a narcissistic bully; he had always thought that Rebecca had provoked and disrespected him and that she had compelled Sohail to behave that way.

After Catalina passed her driving test, she started taking Karina to school. She also learned how to use the GPS, go shopping, and do pretty much whatever she wanted. She was able to make friends without Sohail's help and even socialize in the Filipino community.

Chapter 8

THREE YEARS LATER:

Catalina had fully assimilated herself into her new situation and was becoming more and more confident and independent. She had become the primary driver in the family even when Sohail was in the car. He preferred being a passenger and not having to drive having driven all his life. Catalina felt free and was proud of her independence. Many people told her that she had learned things faster than normal for people coming to the United States, and Sohail took pride in the progress she had made.

Josh remembered that one main reason Sohail wanted to get involved with women from Asian countries was that he did not want one who would become too independent.

"Sohail, do you ever think about what could happen if Catalina didn't need you anymore? I hope that never happens, but that was your primary concern as I recall."

"Josh, I used to think that. What can I say? I was stupid. I can admit that. I mean, look at her. She's been here for almost three years, and she's never given me any reason to complain. I'm so blessed. I'm really happy with my decision. My life is so much better. And Karina is such a joy. I don't know what I'd do without them."

"I'm really happy for you, Sohail. I hope it stays that way," Josh said sincerely.

"Really Josh, I've never seen any red flags. She's such a devoted mother and wife. I've told you that human beings are basically nice, and that belief of mine is getting stronger as time goes on."

Josh smiled. *"Good for you, my friend. I just don't want you to get hurt again."*

"Thanks, Josh. I know you mean well. I've also given it some thought. You know, practically speaking, she's still basically dependent on me, don't you think? I mean not only just financially, but there are other things like, say, health insurance. You probably don't know this, but she's extremely health conscious. I just can't believe that she would ever jeopardize her daughter's well-being, I mean, what would she gain by messing things up?"

Sohail knew that Josh was a sincere friend and wanted what was best for him, but he also knew that Josh was still skeptical only because of his and Catalina's age difference.

Both of them remembered that there was a bet going on, and that they were nearing the half way mark, but neither wanted to address that subject.

Chapter 9

Leona hated the fact that everyone in Catalina's family was raving about how she had beaten the odds and how happy she was. Whenever someone brought that subject up, she'd cringe; it bugged the hell out of her. She felt she had to somehow bring her sister down in a way that no one would expect her of having had anything to do with. After going over and over the matter for months, she came up with an idea though she realized it was a long shot.

She remembered that George Mendoza, a former classmate, had immigrated to the United States after he had dumped her and Catalina many years earlier; both sisters had had a crush on George. He was very good looking and he knew it. He also knew that Leona and Catalina liked him. He had played both sisters and then took advantage of them. He later dumped them both and married a rich girl, who had taken him to the United States. Leona remembered that Catalina was really heartbroken when she found out that he had moved to the States.

Leona searched for him on Facebook and found about a dozen George Mendozas. She went through their profiles and found who she thought was him. She figured there was no harm in contacting him though she wasn't sure it was the George she had in mind. She sent him a friend request, which was quickly accepted. She then messaged him.

"George, this is Leona, we went to school together in Manila, Catalina's sister, do you remember me?"

"Oh yeah yeah, I remember you. How are you? Wow, what a surprise. I can't believe it. How is Catalina? Gosh it's been so many years."

George was excited to hear from someone in Philippines.

"Yes almost twenty years. How have you been? How is the married life? How many kids, how old are they?" Leona bombarded him with questions.
"Well, I am not married any longer."

That perked up Leona interest immediately.

"My marriage didn't last long. Actually less than a year, and of course I don't have any kids.".
"Wow, less than a year? So sorry to hear that."

George opened up to Leona; his wife was living with her parents, and he had never gotten along with his ex father-in-law, a corporate executive. He said that the old man kept getting him involved in the office-type desk jobs that did not suit his personality.

"He and I just never saw eye to eye. The man never understood that there are people in this world who are not cut out for an office job. To him, it was all about money. His philosophy was that if you are making a good salary, you shouldn't complain, just be grateful. Shut up and do what your boss tells you. I am not that type of person, so we had many arguments. To him, my not being interested in that kind of a job meant that I was lazy and not ambitious. During these conflicts, I expected my wife to support me and take my side. That didn't happen. Instead, she was always making excuses for her dad, so I just gave up and left. Good thing that it happened early in the marriage and we didn't have any kids."

Leona was really impressed by how he had stood up to his father-in-law and his wife's demands until he really shocked her even more.

"You know, Leona, what my dream job was and still is?"

"What? Tell me!"

"I always wanted to live and work in Las Vegas."

"Oh my God, really George? The famous Las Vegas? I have heard so much about it. People in the Philippines talk about it as if it were a fantasy island. Isn't that where they have a lot of gambling and there were so many movies made about it?"

"That's it, you got it. Actually it's a desert, not an island."

"How close did you get to your dream job?"

"Believe it or not, you're messaging someone who is right now in Las Vegas."

"Whaaat? Are you serious? You are in Las Vegas right now? What do you do there?"

"I have a dream job. I'm a card dealer in a casino in Vegas and couldn't be happier."

"Wow! George, that is really something. I can't believe I am talking to somebody in the famous Las Vegas. I am so impressed. There aren't too many people in this world who are that lucky. I mean, wow! You're living where you wanted to live and doing the job you wanted. That's really amazing."

"So how about Catalina? How is she? Is she still in Manila? You guys live close by?"

"Now it's now my turn to surprise you."

"Surprise me. Hope she's all right."

"She's also in the United States."

"What? Really? Where? What state?"

"California. I think she is in Los Angeles. Is that in California? How far is California from where you are?"

"California is a border state. It is very close to where I am, and Los Angeles is not far at all. It is only a few hours' drive. Maybe I can visit her sometime."

Leona couldn't believe her ears. Her whole purpose in looking for George was to somehow stir the pot in Catalina's life. She had just found out that George was single, lived not too far from Catalina, and was even willing to visit her. *This couldn't get any better. Now's the perfect time to put ideas in his head*, she thought. Instead of telling him how happy Catalina was, she started painting a totally opposite picture of her sister's situation.

"You know, George, Catalina has had a lot of tragedies in her life. Her first marriage ended up in a divorce in Manila. Her husband used to drink heavily and beat her up."

"Oh wow, that's terrible."

"After putting up with him as much as she could, they finally divorced. After that bitter divorce, she and her daughter came back home to live with my parents. Her husband didn't care much about her, but he loved his daughter. Catalina had a hard time getting full custody of her. She had to hire a lawyer, which was expensive."

"Poor Catalina. Hope your father helped her."

"My father was going through a rough time with his business and had lost a lot of money. He couldn't support Catalina and her daughter for very long, so he basically got her married to this rich old guy. This guy is twice her age and lives in California. That's

where she is now, and I am sure she is miserable there. Poor Catalina—her first husband beat her up, and her second husband is twice her age. Of course she is not happy. How could she be? She pretends to be happy so that my parents don't worry."

"Wow. I am really sorry to hear that, Leona. It must be tough."

"You know I was really upset with my dad. He basically sold his daughter to a stranger who was not only so much older but also lived in a foreign country. Worst of all, she knew no one there. This guy is older than my father, he is from a completely different background, different culture, different religion. Poor Catalina not only takes care of herself but also a little girl who had to leave her school in the Philippines. Poor little girl had to leave all her friends behind in Manila and start all over again. You know something else, that creep has his own children and grandchildren. His children are older than Catalina. My father basically sold my sister to that old son of a bitch just because he had money. I don't understand him. How could he do this to his own daughter just because of money?"

Leona was now emphasizing on the money aspect.

"So the old guy is really rich? Huh!"

"Yeah, from what we hear from Catalina, they have a huge house and many cars and whatnot. I never liked the guy from day one. At his age, he should be sitting at home and enjoying the rest of his days with his children and grandchildren. Not this guy—he had to have a young woman take care of him."

"Leona, you should give me her number. I will give her a call. Maybe it will cheer her up a little bit."

"I will. I think she will be really glad to hear from you. It will be a nice surprise, but don't tell her that I gave you her number."

"Okay, I won't."

The next day, Leona gave him Catalina's number.

Chapter 10

Leona was encouraged by George's willingness to listen to her lies and exaggerations. She knew she was making headway toward her goal of causing trouble in Catalina's marriage.

Leona and George talked often after that initial conversation. She repeated her assertions every chance she got about the evil old man who had successfully bought another human being, her sister. She repeatedly reminded him about he had dangled money in front of her father and had talked him into making that decision.

She deliberately did not tell George that her father had been the one who had posted ads on the site with pictures of Catalina that Sohail had responded to and that that was how they had met. Instead, she continuously bad-mouthed Sohail.

"What a wicked man he must be to want to buy a wife half his age. He was so selfish he didn't even care about how embarrassing it must be for Catalina to introduce him to everybody as her husband. She looked like his daughter and how confusing it must be for poor little Karina."

Leona figured out that George and she had one thing in common—a propensity to cause trouble—and her instincts to create trouble were at their peak; she knew how to incite and exploit the situation. She always told George how sorry she felt for her sister and how she wished she could rescue her sweet, dear sister from that old man's clutches.

Her jealousy and animosity for her sister had no boundaries knowing how everyone in her family was raving about her. Everyone had seen Catalina suffer at the hands of her ex-husband and thought that she deserved her newly acquired happiness.

Leona repeatedly instructed George not to tell anyone, including Catalina, that she was in touch with him.

"You see George, no matter what she went through, Catalina is still a proud woman. She would not want you, an outsider, to sympathize with her."

Leona told George repeatedly how filthy rich Sohail was and how Catalina was living in a mansion and driving expensive cars. That piqued George's interest even more.

He was single, and he remembered that Catalina was quite pretty. From the first time Leona had told him about Catalina's story, he had already started imagining being with a pretty Filipino woman with lots of money.

It didn't take long for Leona to figure out which of George's buttons to push.

Chapter 11

At the first opportunity, George called Catalina's land line, and Sohail picked up.

"Hello?"

"Hello, is Catalina there?"

"Yes she is. Who's calling? This is her husband."

"Can I speak to her? I'm an old friend of hers from the Philippines. We went to school together."

"Oh, okay. Let me get her."

Catalina was in the kitchen, and Sohail asked her to pick up the extension.

"Hey Catalina, this is George Mendoza. You remember me? I went to school with you and Leona."

"Oh yeah, I remember you of course. Where are you? How's your wife, and how many kids do you have? How nice of you to call." Catalina was excited. "By the way, how did you get my number?"

"That's too many questions in one breath, I don't even know where to begin with them."

That made Catalina laugh. "You're the same funny George I knew. Okay, how about this. Where are you calling from? Somebody told me you went to the United States."

"Yes I did, and I'm still there."

"Which state?"

"Nevada. I'm in Las Vegas, not far from you."

"Oh wow! I know where it is. In that case, you and your wife should come and visit. I'd love for you to meet my husband, Sohail, and my daughter, Karina."

Sohail was listening intently.

"*What if I tell you I don't have a wife? Will the invitation still stand?*" George asked laughing.

"*You're joking, right?*"

"*No, I'm not married. My wife and I divorced shortly after we were married, and we didn't have any kids.*"

George brought Catalina up to date with himself.

"*Oh wow. Sorry to hear that, George.*"

"*Don't be. I'm very happy. I'm in the United States, and I have the best job in the world. I live in Las Vegas, a place where half the world dreams of visiting. What else could a man ask for?*"

Catalina told him about herself adding toward the end that she was also very happy with her new family, which brought a smile to Sohail's face.

George didn't believe that after what Leona had told him; he assumed she was saying it only because her husband was around.

"*So what about that invitation? Is it still good?*"

Catalina started speaking in Tagalog, the Filipino language. That perked up Sohail's ears; he didn't understand a word. He had heard her say that he was unmarried. Sohail also heard her give the caller her cell number.

Chapter 12

As soon as she was done talking, he let her know he was upset.

"Why did you switch to Tagalog in the middle of a conversation? Did you not want me to know what you were talking about?"

"No, no, of course not. It's just that when two Filipinos talk, they're more comfortable speaking their native language."

"I thought everyone spoke English in the Philippines. Isn't English your language?"

"They do. But they prefer to speak Tagalog among friends."

"Well, you were talking in English at first. Weren't you friends then? What? All of a sudden you remembered you were friends, so you wanted to speak in Tagalog? And how good of a friend is—I mean, was—he?"

"Sohail, I can't believe this. You've never talked to me like this before."

"And you've never acted like this before. A married woman talking to an unmarried man who lives in Las Vegas. All of a sudden you switch to a language your husband doesn't understand, and I was standing next to you. That to me was very disrespectful. And oh, by the way, what was the reason for giving him your cell number may I ask?"

Catalina started crying. *"I didn't know that my old schoolmate's calling me would upset you so much. I told him it was okay for him to come for dinner. I wanted him to meet you and Karina."*

Sohail got even more upset that she had invited him over without having talked to him first. *"Call him back right now and tell him your husband doesn't want him to come! And next time, make sure to talk to me first before inviting people over."*

Catalina couldn't believe her ears; the same Sohail, who had always been so nice and kind to her, was talking to her like that. He had never been so upset; she hadn't seen that side of him.

She did what she had been told. She called George back in front of Sohail and told him in English not to come; she hung up right away. She didn't want to explain to him what had happened and why she was taking back the invitation. She looked at Sohail to see if he was satisfied. He seemed to her to be. She went upstairs to their bedroom, closed the door, and started sobbing again.

It was day time and Karina was at school.

After that incident, George was convinced that Leona had been right about the old man and that Catalina was living under great duress. He was convinced she was totally under his control and had no freedom to do anything on her own, not even to invite anyone over. He was totally convinced that she needed his help.

Sohail on the other hand was also not happy about how things had transpired. He called Josh to tell him what had happened and to get his advice.

"Hey Josh. You ready for this? I just saw the first red flag."

"What? What happened?" Josh heard some anxiousness in Sohail's voice.

Sohail told him exactly what had happened, but Josh disagreed that it was a red flag; he thought it was a knee-jerk reaction on Sohail's part.

"Do you even know what a red flag means? Why do you think this was a red flag? She was inviting an old friend to her house for dinner. You and your daughter would be

there, so what's the problem? She wanted him to meet her family. For God's sake, this guy was not an ordinary friend. He was her schoolmate from her native land. It's not that she was going to meet him at a motel or meet him behind your back. I just don't see where you're coming from."

"So why would she start speaking in Tagalog in the middle of their conversation unless she wanted to hide something from me?"

"I've heard people from other countries switch to their native languages without even knowing they're doing that, no matter how long they've lived here. Haven't you done that yourself?"

Sohail realized Josh was right, but then he thought of something else. "Okay, wise guy, why would she give him her cell number?"

"You've gone nuts in your old age, Sohail. Nowadays, even five-year-olds have their own cell phones. Haven't you noticed nobody uses landlines anymore? Not everybody is old school like you. I don't have a landline. I got sick of answering telemarketers and robocalls on that line.

You have any more stupid questions? I have to get back to work. Go and apologize to her. Better yet, buy her some flowers first. Talk to you later, genius."

It had taken Josh no time at all to make Sohail realize how wrong he had been with his suspicions.

He went upstairs. Catalina was still sobbing. He hugged her and apologized to her.

"Look, sweetheart, I've been thinking. I realize I was wrong. I'm sorry."

She forgave him right away. "Sohail, I've been thinking too. I understand why you are so sensitive. It's because of what happened with your first marriage."

Sohail was happy and grateful that it had taken so little effort to get Catalina to forgive him. He remembered how long and difficult it used to be for him and Rebecca to reconcile when they got into conflicts; it used to take forever even when he was convinced he was right.

Catalina told Sohail all about George. When Sohail found out that not only was he single but he was also a card dealer, he told her she would be better off staying away from him.

Chapter 13

Both Sohail and Catalina expected George to contact her again on her cell, and sure enough he did. She knew better than to talk to him; she immediately handed her phone to Sohail, who told him, *"Look, mister, please don't call her anymore. She doesn't want to talk to you."*

"Why? She's an adult, and this is America. You can't control her like that!" George confronted Sohail.

"Look, you idiot, I'm not controlling her. It's her choice. She's a married woman, and she doesn't want to associate with someone like you."

"Someone like me? What do you mean, you old goat?" George counterattacked.

"Get the fuck out of my face, you asshole! Next time you call her, we'll call the police and report harassment." Then he hung up.

Catalina was shocked to hear all that; she was not used to such drama, and she felt she had been the cause of all this commotion.

George was then even more convinced that Leona had been right and that Catalina was in the shackles of this old man. He called Leona and told her what had happened.

Leona was delirious with joy; she couldn't believe how well her plan was working. She was as happy as she could be, but she was careful not to let George know that.

"See? What did I tell you, George? That old man is an evil, tyrannical, and spiteful person. I wish I could do something about that bastard and help my dear sister. I feel so helpless sitting here so far away. George, you're our only hope. I don't know what else to say."

"Don't worry, Leona. I have a very good understanding of what's going on. I wish I could somehow just talk to her privately. I have to figure out how I can talk to her when the old man isn't around. I'll keep trying—Don't worry. I must help her. I think she needs my help very badly."

George had no clue of the games Leona was playing and how she had suckered him completely. She was smart enough to realize that the iron was hot, that she must do something quickly.

"I just got an idea, George. I'll find out what time she drops off and picks up Karina from school and let you know. How's that?"

"That's great! Also, give me her address. I want to know where she lives." George started seeing some hope of meeting Catalina alone and seeing what kind of house she lived in.

"Okay. Give me a few days." Leona was thrilled that she had found a solution.

When Sohail and Catalina didn't hear from George for a few days, they were glad and were hoping they would never hear from him again.

Like most immigrants who come to the United States, Catalina was in touch with her family regularly using WhatsApp, Facebook, Skype, and so on. It didn't take long for Leona to find out the information she needed to give to George.

Chapter 14

Not long after George found out from Leona where Catalina lived, he headed for Los Angeles. His motives were dubious. On one hand, he was going to be the savior of an innocent woman who was in the clutches of a cruel, barbarous, wicked old man. On the other hand, he also wanted to see his old girlfriend, who was rich. Leona had told him so many times about how rich Sohail was, and George thought that if he could convince Catalina to leave him, he could have the girl *and* the money. *How sweet would that be?* he asked himself.

Leona had told him that Karina's school started at 8:30. He figured Catalina probably left home at 8:15. He made sure he was near her house at 8:00, and sure enough, he spotted her and followed her to the school. When she got back to her car after dropping off Karina, he was there in front of her.

"Hello, Catalina!"

She was totally flabbergasted.

"Oh my God! Is that you, George? I can't believe it! I'm seeing you in the flesh and blood. Wow! Sorry about all the commotion a few days ago." They hugged. Catalina flashed back to when she had dated him—how good looking he was, how he smelled. She was spellbound. For the next few seconds, she forgot she was a married woman and a mother.

George tried to tell her, that he understood that she was in a tight situation, and that she doesn't have much control over what was going on with her husband.

"I'm really sorry you have to live under such circumstances, but hopefully, it won't be for too long."

Catalina didn't understand what he meant by that, but she was too excited to ask him. She was seeing somebody who had been her first love after almost twenty years. She also knew that she had only a few minutes before she had to head home. She told George she had to leave soon, which made George sad.

"When can I see you again for a little bit longer so we can talk and catch up? Can you call me when you can get away?"

"No, I can't. Sohail can check my phone." Then she thought about it for a minute.

"The only thing I can do is tell Sohail that I'm going shopping tomorrow after dropping off Karina. You can meet me here at the same time. I have to go. See you tomorrow."

They hugged again, and she quickly left.

On her way home, she was so nervous that she barely avoided running into another car. The combination of her guilt and fear was overwhelming. Sohail was home. She avoided any eye contact with him all day and just kept herself busy.

George was beyond himself too. He was so happy that all his plans were working. Exactly as he had hoped, Catalina had been happy to see him. He thought it couldn't get any better than that. She was even willing to see him behind her husband's back.

He called Leona to let her know how well everything had gone, and she was thrilled that her plans and maneuvering were working. She was indeed stirring the pot, but she didn't like the fact that Catalina would get to spend more time with George.

The next day, George was waiting for Catalina. As soon as she dropped off Karina, he asked her to park her car close by, and he took her to a coffee shop. He was clever enough to take a selfie with her just in case. He told her that he wanted to talk about something important. He took her to the hotel where he was staying.

Catalina was extremely nervous to the point that she was shaking. George noticed that and tried to calm her down. He convinced himself that she was shaking because of her nervousness and was frightened of her husband. *After all, the bastard has been torturing her for so long.*

While calming her down, he was also embracing and comforting her. Pretty soon he started kissing her. She was in such a state of confusion that when George started making advances, she didn't stop him, which encouraged him. Pretty soon, he was unbuttoning her blouse, and he still met no resistance.

Sohail had told her from the outset of their marriage that he was too old for any sexual activity, and Catalina had been divorced for a number of years before meeting Sohail.

She was more confused after they made love. So many different thoughts were going through her head. There were plenty of flashbacks too of how they had been together years earlier.

In the meantime, George was lying next to her, happy as could be. He had no idea what kind of commotion was going on in the person's head lying next to him.

"Everything okay? What are you thinking?" George asked as he kissed her cheek. *"You've been so quiet."*

Catalina suddenly got up and shook herself off. The combination of nervousness and guilt was too much for her to bear; she felt as if her head was going to explode. She couldn't take it anymore. She immediately decided that she must get away. She told George that she wasn't feeling well and wanted to leave right away. George didn't believe her, but he knew that Sohail's hold and influence over her was so powerful that she couldn't help herself.

George was smart enough not to resist her and go slowly. He unsuccessfully tried to tell her that everything was okay, but she had made up her mind to leave. He just tried to comfort her and dropped her off at school by her car. He tried one more time to embrace her and give her a kiss, but she pushed him away and sped off, telling him never to contact her again.

George was shocked, totally blown away by the sudden change; he couldn't figure out what had happened. They had been making love just a few minutes earlier, and she had given him no indication that he was doing anything against her will, and then *Bam!!*

Something had triggered. He again blamed it on her husband's power and his total grip over her mind.

Chapter 15

Sohail was watching TV when Catalina walked in and burst into tears. She was crying at the top of her lungs. Sohail had no clue as to what had happened.

"What happened? Why are you crying? Sweetheart, please tell me what happened. Did somebody hurt you? Say something to you? Were you in an accident?"

"Sohail, I've done something so stupid that I'm afraid you'll never forgive me!"

"What can it be that has you crying so hysterically? Come on please tell me."

"I saw George. Somehow, he found out where we lived and where Karina's school was."

"WHAT?" Sohail was furious. *"YOU DID WHAT? You met him in spite of knowing how I felt about him? In spite of what happened on the phone the other day?"*

Catalina's guilt and shame were so overwhelming that she just kept looking down.

Sohail was shaking his spinning head. *"I don't know what to say ... What to do!"*

Catalina was still sobbing uncontrollably. *"I don't know what happened to me. Everything happened so fast. As soon as I saw him, all my memories of him flashed back. He was so nice. I just remembered my past with him, and everything else blacked out! Sohail, I want to be totally honest with you and let you know everything that happened. When we were departing and he tried to come close to me, I pushed him away and told him never to contact me again."*

"Now it's up to you. You decide whether to believe me

or not. Do what you want to do. I admit I did something really, really stupid and deserve everything coming to me."

She then headed to the bedroom.

Sohail called the police.

"We want to file a report against a man who's harassing our family. His name is George Mendoza. He keeps calling my wife in spite of her telling him not to. Although he lives in Las Vegas, he has come to Los Angeles just to harass us. He went to high school with my wife back in the Philippines. Somehow, he found out our address. He even got the address of our child's school and went there this morning to harass my wife. We believe he'll go to the school again in spite of the fact she's told him never to contact her."

The police took all the information and told him that they would keep an eye on their house and the school. Sohail gave them the house and school's addresses and Catalina's license plate.

Sohail was beyond angry and confused. This was a sudden jolt he hadn't been expecting. The only thing he could think of was to call Josh and get his advice.

"Hey Josh, I really need your help. This time, it's way more than a red flag."

Sohail sounded confused and angry to Josh.

"First of all, calm down. Tell me what happened. You sound weird."

"After my last phone call with George, I thought the fucker had gone away since we hadn't heard from him for a while. But no. Somehow, he found out where we live and even where Karina's school was. Can you believe it?"

"Whaaat?"

"Yes! Now you understand why I sound weird?"

"What did he do? How did she react? She must have been scared."

"No, she didn't get scared. She was apparently thrilled to see him. She blamed it on flashbacks, memories of him. She went to the coffee shop with him and even to his room. Then she had the nerve to come home and tell me everything. Can you believe it? Now she's crying hysterically. I don't know what to do, man. I'm totally bummed out."

"What did you say to her? What did you do?"

"I don't know what to do with her, but I did call the police to let them know that this man was a danger to my family and was harassing my wife."

Josh agreed with Sohail's decision to call the police, but he also asked Sohail to think about everything rationally and make sure to avoid any knee-jerk reactions.

"Look, Sohail, I agree initially it doesn't look good, that she met with another man and went to his hotel room. But try to look at the circumstances realistically. He was not just any man. We're talking about her first boyfriend. I'm sure even you know the impact that your first love in life can have on a person. Remember, she hadn't seen him in twenty-some years.

"She'd gone to school with him, but this time, she was seeing him in a different country, and she probably got overwhelmed. Most likely, the flashbacks were so powerful and overwhelming that she temporarily forgot that she was a married woman and a mother. As soon as she came to her senses and realized her mistake, she got away from him. Then she told him to not contact her again. If she wanted to continue meeting with him, why would she tell him not to contact her again? Here's something you should consider very seriously. If she really was a bad woman and wanted to cheat on you, why would she tell you everything as soon as she got home? I think she definitely deserves the benefit of the doubt.

"Now let me ask you something very personal. You don't have to answer it if you don't want to. But I'll ask it anyway since you're my friend."

"I don't mind, Josh. You know everything about me. I have nothing to hide."

"Are you intimate with her?"

Sohail was taken aback by a question he hadn't expected.

Josh didn't wait for his answer. *"If the answer is no, that's another reason she fell under his spell. It was a basic instinct, a natural human reaction. She didn't have time to think. Look—I'm no psychiatrist or psychologist, but I know this much. Under traumatic situations, a person's memory can become fuzzy and repressed."*

Sohail hadn't expected to hear that, but it made sense. Josh's reasoning was so powerful that it shook him to his core. He appreciated Josh more than ever.

"My wise friend, what can I say? You're right once again. You son of a gun, are you sure you weren't a psychologist or psychiatrist in a previous life?"

"I should start charging you a fee. I've saved your ass so many times, Sohail."

Josh was joshing.

"Without a doubt I admit it. Guilty as charged. Go ahead and send me your bill. I'll be happy to pay it, my friend." Sohail was clearly pleased.

Sohail was so overwhelmed with this pep talk that he vowed to forgive Catalina and pledged with all his heart to start working on his marriage again. He recalled why he had wanted to remarry in the first place and how badly he had wanted to make this marriage work.

He went to Catalina, who was lying on the bed terrified about what Sohail was going to do. He lay down next to her and kissed her cheek. She was surprised and more than pleased. He kept gazing at her silently.

"What? Why are you looking at me like that?"

Sohail knew that she was anxiously waiting to find out what he was going to do. He gave her another kiss on the cheek.

"What are you doing, Sohail? You're confusing me. Does that mean you aren't mad at me and you've forgiven me?"

Sohail embraced her and asked her if his tight embrace answered her question about forgiveness.

Tears started rolling down Catalina's eyes. She was beyond puzzled. She couldn't believe it.

"Sohail, I don't understand you. I just did something so terrible that I thought you'd never forgive me."

He put his finger on her lips and gently stopped her. He then told her how he felt and that he wanted to start all over again. He didn't tell her about his conversation with Josh because he didn't want her to know he had discussed his personal life with an outsider.

"Here I am thinking that you'd never forgive me and you're telling me this?"

"Yes, that's how I feel. I know what you did and why you did it. You temporarily got overwhelmed. He was somebody you really cared for at one time in your life."

"Sohail, you're the most understanding person in the whole world, and you're also the best husband in the world. I love you so, so so much."

It was her turn to embrace him. She started tussling with him until they both fell on the floor. She jumped on him and didn't loosen her grip.

Both were very happy.

Chapter 16

The next day, George went to Karina's school again as expected, and the police were waiting for him. When he tried to talk to Catalina, they grabbed him and took him to the police station. Catalina nervously saw everything.

When she got home after dropping off Karina, she was terrified. She told Sohail how George had tried to talk to her and how he'd been immediately arrested.

Sohail was happy to hear that.

"Good! Maybe they'll put him away for a long time and he'll learn a lesson. At least he'll leave us alone."

But that was wishful thinking on Sohail's part.

That afternoon, the police called Sohail and told him that they had let George go.

"Why? What happened? Why didn't he remain locked up?" Sohail was upset.

"Mr. Kolsy, there was plenty of evidence to prove that your wife was a willful partner in all his actions. He showed us a picture of himself and your wife taken yesterday in which they were smiling and looking happy. We investigated the coffee shop and the hotel where they went. People who saw them at those places didn't see anything unusual or anyone under duress. Mr. Kolsy, please explain to your wife that falsely accusing someone to the police is a very serious charge that could be construed as a felony. The suspect has gone back to Las Vegas. Let us know if he causes you any more trouble."

Sohail didn't know the subtleties of the law, but he was grateful that Catalina hadn't gotten into trouble though it had been close. He thought of all the things that could have gone wrong and was grateful that they had dodged the bullet.

Chapter 17

That was not the first time George had run into trouble with the law, so getting arrested hadn't bothered him too much. He was convinced that Sohail, not Catalina, had called the police on him. He was also convinced that Catalina wanted to see him again but was in Sohail's clutches mentally and physically. In George's mind, Sohail had so much power over her that she could not get out of it and needed rescuing badly. In his mind, he was the only one who knew the whole situation and the only one who could help her. He had to make this his mission.

He told Leona about everything that had happened in Los Angeles and how he got arrested.

"What are we going to do now, George? Now you believe me how evil this man is? I've been telling you all along. My sister's under some kind of spell. I'm even afraid for her life. God forbid—If something happens to her, what will happen to that sweet, innocent child? My parents wouldn't be able to bear it. George, please do something!"

Leona's instigation and incitement was at it's peak.

"Yes, I agree, Leona, something must be done and fast! I'm more determined than ever. I won't rest until I do something about this man. Our sweet Catalina is in danger. I know she's terrified of him. Maybe he beats her up or shows some other kind of cruelty. Let me talk to some people here. I'll get back to you."

Such talk was music to Leona's ears.

By this time, George became obsessed with liberating Catalina from Sohail's clutches.

All kinds of thoughts raced through his mind. He lived in Sin City, where all kinds of people lived. He knew people who had recently been released from prison, people who were in and out of jail frequently, people who were on parole … He also knew people employed by casinos as bouncers whose job it was to keep troublemakers in line.

George was thinking of one guy in particular who worked in the security department of his casino—John Metcalf. He was friendly and easy to talk to. A couple of times when the customers had too much to drink and were getting out of control at his table, John had helped George with them. George asked John if they could meet for coffee after their shift was over, and John agreed.

At the coffee shop, George started by saying, *"John, I have a serious problem and was wondering if you could help me. You won't believe what my ex-girlfriend is going through."*

He told John about his trip to Los Angeles and his arrest; he told him how badly he wanted to save her. *"She's married to this horrible old man twice her age."* He exaggerated his story to gain more sympathy from John by telling him how the old man beats her up and put her in chains.

John was very sympathetic and was surprised that in this day and age, such extreme domestic violence was still happening. He had no reason not to believe George's story. John didn't know George very well, but he sounded convincing. When John asked George how he knew all this, he lied again and said that his ex had told him.

"How come she doesn't report it to the police?"

"She doesn't want to lose the financial security the old man provides, and she needs to take care of her daughter."

After listening to George's story, John asked, *"Do you have a solution? Maybe you can secretly help her financially or get her a lawyer who can get her out of her dilemma."*

George told him that the old man was very rich and had tight security in his house making it extremely difficult to penetrate. He also told John that she still loved George after all these years and wanted to marry him but only if the old man wasn't in their way.

George's last statement startled John, who was no dummy. At first, he had been slightly skeptical, but when he heard that part of the story, he quickly put the two and two together.

"Woah, man. You're talking about a huge crime here. Are you serious you want to do this?"

George was very careful to make this all about Catalina although he was lying. He was also testing John as to what he would say and what his reaction would be.

"Yes, I'm serious. Do you know anybody who could do the job?"

"Not personally, but I could ask around. Something like this would cost a lot of money. How much are you or your ex-girlfriend willing to spend?"

"Like I said, the old man's very rich. We'd be able to pay only after the job was done."

George was still testing John.

"George, it doesn't work that way. Nobody would take a serious hitman's job like this without getting paid in advance."

"Do you have any idea what would it cost? How much we'd have to come up with?"

"I don't know for sure, but my best guess is fifteen to twenty thousand in advance and more after the job's finished."

"That's a lot of money, man. Unfortunately, the old man keeps a tight grip on his cash."

"Well George, I'll check around and get back to you. You stay out of trouble, you hear?"

George was glad that he had found an ally who would at least listen to his woes and give him some ideas.

He called Leona with this new development; keeping her in the loop made him feel good. He also thought of her as an ally who could come up with ideas herself. Leona was also helpful with information about Catalina and what her family was thinking.

Although John Metcalf was working in the security department at the casino, unbeknown to George, he had other career ambitions. He wanted to become a detective in the Las Vegas Police Department. George had just given him an excellent opportunity to get into the good graces of the police department as a confidential source for future employment reference. He immediately reported this incident to the Las Vegas Metropolitan Police Department (LVMPD).

"Can I speak to the supervisor of the homicide bureau?"

"This is Detective Mercer. I'm the supervisor. How can I help you?"

"My name's John Metcalf. I'm a security officer at Windsor Casino, and I'd like to report a potential homicidal plan that someone's cooking up."

"What kind of plan? How do you know about it? Do you have any witnesses, any evidence?"

"Yes I do."

"What kind of evidence? Did you personally hear him say anything?"

"Not only did I hear it, but the suspect was actually talking to me. He asked me to find a hitman for him."

"In that case, John, I'd like to meet with you. Will that be okay?"

"Sure."

"Can you text me your address and phone number?"

"Sure."

Chapter 18

Detective Steve Mercer, age forty-seven and a veteran detective, had recently been promoted to supervisor. As an undercover agent, he had handled dozens of similar homicide cases.

Before meeting with John Metcalf, the detective started a case file and assigned it a case number per department policy.

He then met with John and thanked him for his timely reporting of a potentially serious crime. Mercer let John know that he was an undercover agent and gave him his cell number.

"Please give it to George and ask him to contact me directly."

"Will do," John said. He quickly added, *"Just want to let you know, Detective Mercer, that this guy doesn't have much money. From what I can gather, he likes good stuff and spends everything he earns."*

"Thanks. Good to know that. Considering that, you can tell him he's lucky that you found him somebody who'll do the job cheap."

John was happy that he was in the good graces of the LVMPD. He was sure that it would be good for his future employment reference. He was definitely planning on applying for a detective's position in the near future.

John called George the next day. *"Hey man, how're you doing?"*

"What's up, John? You have any good news for me?"

"Yeah, man. You're in luck. I found somebody, and the cost will be a lot less than what I originally thought. I better give you the information in person. It's probably not safe to talk on the phone. Look, I feel really bad for your girlfriend. It's not right what she's going through. That old

man seems real evil." John wanted to convince George that his cause was noble and that he had found an ally in John.

"*Yeah man, that's why I am taking such a big risk.*" George liked what John was saying.

They met at the same coffee shop where they had met earlier, and John gave George Mercer's phone number. When George asked him how much money he needed to have, John told him to just call Mercer.

George called Mercer the first chance he got. At first, they both started talking in code language.

"*Hello. John Metcalf asked me to call you. Can you do the job?*"

"*Yes of course, but are you sure you want to do this? If it's not done right, the punishment can be extremely severe. You know that, right?*"

"*Hey man, I don't want any lectures from you. Just tell me how much it's going to cost me.*" George wanted to sound like a tough guy.

"*Five thousand dollars upfront. Not a penny less. John must have told you that that's very cheap for this kind of a job.*"

George was happy that John had been right; Mercer was much cheaper than he had expected.

"*What kind of experience do you have? How many operations like this have you done before?*"

"*More than you want to know, buddy. That's why I'm so cheap.*"

"*Okay, let me get back to you.*"

"*Whatever. You know how to contact me.*" Mercer was very cool.

Detective Mercer wrote an official report of their phone call that went into the case file. Based on this official LVMPD report, they would be able to get authorization from a Las Vegas judge to surveil George's telephone activities.

George called Leona after meeting with Mercer.

"Hey, Leona, I have good news and bad news. Which do you want hear first?"

"I can use some good news."

"I've found someone who can do the job. It's not going to be fifteen thousand like our initial information was. It'll be much cheaper. The guy wants only a third of that. The guy sounds real professional and seems like he knows what he's talking about. He came highly recommended by somebody I know personally."

Leona couldn't believe how fast George was moving.

"Okay, so what's the bad news?"

"The bad news is that I have only four thousand saved up and I am one thousand short."

Leona was so much involved in the plan that she wanted to put up the remaining thousand, but that was a lot of money in the Philippines; she had only about six hundred saved up. She told George that she would see if she could borrow the remaining $400 from a friend and would call him the next day.

Sure enough, Leona called George the next day and told him she had gotten the $400.

Everything Leona and George said was being recorded.

Catalina and Sohail were happy that they hadn't heard from George since he had left for Las Vegas. They hoped they would never hear from him again.

Sohail had completely forgiven Catalina. After that episode with George, they had pledged to each other that they would do everything to make their marriage stronger.

A week later, George called Mercer.

"Hi, this is George Mendoza. We talked last week."

"Yeah, I remember you."

"I want to meet with you and want to know the details. I want to know everything about how you're going to make this happen."

"Do you have the money?"

"Yes."

Again, the conversation was being taped.

Mercer asked him to meet him at the same coffee shop. He wanted to make George as comfortable as possible.

As his training required, Mercer started preparing to meet a potentially dangerous criminal. It was always a psychological dual that demanded training as well as instinct. After studying George's profile he had developed based on what John Metcalf had told him, he knew he was about to meet a man who was dangerous. Anyone who did not have any remorse and was willing to get another human being killed for personal gain was obviously very dangerous.

When Mercer met with George, he took his partner, Philip Turner, with him for more evidence and to be a witness. Mercer was also wearing a wire.

When George showed up, he was startled to see Philip. *"I didn't know you were going to bring an unknown person into this conversation."*

"Hey man, don't worry about Phil. He works for me, and we always work together. I need his help. We've done dozens of operations like this as a team." Mercer assured George that he always needs a partner for this kind of dangerous work.

George reluctantly agreed, but he said as sternly as he could, *"I need to know all the details about your plan, how you're going to start and finish the job. There's a lot on the line here for me."*

Mercer again told him that he'd had a lot of experience in this kind of work and particularly in the Los Angeles area. He told George that the way it worked was that they would surveil the target for about a month to establish the pattern of his movements.

"We gotta find out when the target leaves his house, where he goes, how often, and all his movements. Once the pattern is established, that's when Phil and I'll look for the right opportunity to act. There's a drug called scopolamine that's very effective in this kind of operation. We've used it dozens of times. One of us will silently go behind the target and grab him. After the target sniffs it, he'll be unconscious in seconds."

George then insisted on knowing what Mercer would do with the body. Mercer was ready for that question. He told George that he was very familiar with plenty of abandoned dumping grounds in and around Los Angeles. The body will be disposed off in one of those dumping grounds and nobody would ever find it.

Mercer was answering all George's questions so confidently that George was almost ready to give him the green light. But he suddenly got scared when he realized he was about to have somebody killed. *"What if something goes wrong?"*

Mercer was ready for that question too.

"That's the risk we all take? Don't we?" Mercer asked.

When George heard the word *we*, he felt a little better. He had assurance that he was not in it by himself. Then he asked one last question about the timing as to when the plan would be executed.

"Look, man, I'd be lying to you if I told you I could do it tomorrow. Like I said, we gotta do the surveillance and learn the target's patterns. That's vitally important.

These things take time. One mistake and we could face dire consequences."

George seemed satisfied and asked if he could give half the money then and half after the job was finished. Mercer told him that although he had initially asked for the $5,000 upfront, since he seemed like a nice guy, he would agree to split the payment.

George gave Mercer $2,500, which Philip witnessed. Mercer deliberately said very clearly, *"Okay, George, you're giving us twenty-five hundred now and promise to pay us the balance later—is that correct?"*

"Yes, of course," George replied.

They all shook hands and left the coffee shop.

George was proud of himself. He'd gotten those bastards to split the payment and to tell him their exact plans. He was happy that Catalina would soon be out of the clutches of that evil old man and would be in his arms. He'd be a wealthy man, and they'd live a happy life ever after.

In his mind he was sure that the old man must have made arrangements to leave behind everything for Catalina and Karina in case something happened to him.

He called Leona. *"Guess what? Everything's going the way we wanted. I met the guy. He told me everything about how they're going to take care of that old bastard. Aren't you proud of me?"*

"Of course I am, George. What a great job! I hope everything goes according to our plans. I'm so happy for my sister and my niece."

Leona sounded happy, but she wasn't thrilled. In her evil mind, she was thinking that if George succeeded in his plans, her sister would still get to live the rich life in the United States but this time with George, who was the love of her life.

She did take some consolation in thinking she'd be successful in creating havoc in Catalina's life and could hang on to this dark secret and use it to blackmail her if the need arose.

George had no clue about Leona's intentions, and how she actually felt about her sister. He figured she was trying to help her sister and her niece.

Detective Mercer wrote another official report about his meeting with George and the exchange of money. That time, his report was even more solid with Philip as witness and with the tape recording. With that evidence, the LVMPD had a solid case to present to the government prosecutor.

Now, George himself, not just his phone, was under government surveillance; his every move was being tracked. He had no idea the government had built a case against him that was so solid that it was just a matter of time before he would be arrested. He was cluelessly going about his business working at the casino, talking to Leona, and thinking that his life was soon about to dramatically change for the better.

The Philippines law enforcement authorities had been contacted by the LVMPD and were informed of Leona's criminal activities. They were also informed that the extradition paperwork was in process. It took about four weeks for the government to get all the necessary paperwork in order and get the arrest warrant ready. The charge for Leona's extradition was her involvement in the conspiracy to murder Sohail.

Chapter 19

At 4:00 one morning, a day after the paperwork was finished, George was arrested; the charge was to plan and conspire a premeditated murder by hiring two undercover agents. He was immediately read his Miranda rights. *"You have the right to remain silent. Anything you say can and will be used against you in court of law. You have the right to an attorney ..."*

George was stunned; he silently gave himself up.

The Philippines law enforcement authorities was sent the necessary paperwork electronically. They were bound by the extradition treaty signed by the government of Philippines and the government of United States in November 1994. They promptly arrested Leona. The treaty required them to bring Leona to the United States and have her stand trial on criminal charges.

Once George and Leona were in jail, the local government was required to inform the potential victims.

When Sohail and Catalina found out what had been going on behind their backs, they were beyond shocked; they could not believe that things had gone that far. The most shocking part was that Leona had been so deeply involved in the plot. Nobody could have imagined that a family member could do such a thing to another family member.

"How can my own flesh and blood do this to me?" Catalina asked her parents over and over. The rest of the family had been devastated by Leona's actions. Nobody had imagined she could be that callous and cold-blooded. Everyone was concerned about Leona's children. Catalina had always suspected that Leona had had a jealous streak, but it had been beyond her wildest imagination that her jealousy could have gone that far.

Chapter 20

Catalina, Sohail, and Josh attended the trials every day. Catalina was given the opportunity to ask for leniency for her sister, but she refused; she did not think Leona deserved any sympathy from her. Sohail and Josh urged Catalina to at least think about it before rejecting it outright, but she refused.

Sohail and Josh and even her parents told her, *"Please don't forget she has children. Who's going to take care of them?"*

But Catalina wouldn't budge. *"Let their dad take care of them, let their uncles and aunts take care of them, but I don't have an iota of sympathy for that woman. I'll have nothing to do with her ever again. I don't even want to hear her name. She doesn't exist as far as I'm concerned."*

George was sentenced to sixteen years in prison, and Leona received twelve years. She was given the option of serving her time in the Philippines, which she accepted.

Chapter 21

SIX MONTHS LATER:

Josh and Katie hosted a party for Sohail and Catalina to celebrate their seventh anniversary. They also invited Sameera and Salim. Everybody knew that Sohail had gone through a death threat, and they all knew that his and Catalina's marriage was stronger than ever.

Sohail's grandchildren had missed their doting grandpa, and Sameera and Salim had missed their father's love tremendously. They had misunderstood Catalina; they had viewed her as a gold digger and assumed she would show her true colors sooner or later and leave their father.

No such thing had happened. They all had developed a deep respect for Catalina. Her family values and dedication to her daughter and husband were unquestionable.

Chapter 22

Josh had lost the bet. He paid up. They had agreed not to tell anyone, including their wives, about the bet. Sohail was happy to give the check to Catalina so she and Karina could go on a shopping spree.

Everyone was happy and celebrated the occasion until the wee hours.

Printed in the United States
by Baker & Taylor Publisher Services